Stop and Go

For Charlie

Written and created by
Paul Shuttleworth

Edited by **Jill Findlay**

Based on the TV series Harry and Toto
and the TV Script "Stop and Go" written by Paul Shuttleworth
performed by Bob Golding and Sue Devaney
with the music of Liz Kitchen

Original design by
Marcin Wasilewski
Robert Jaszczurowski
Łukasz Kacprowicz

Additional design and book layout by
SunHouse Creative

With special thanks to Loretta Cocchi, Nigel Gamble and BBC Worldwide
toge

Opposite Town is a very friendly place.
Everyone stops to think about others.

There's Opposite Town's Police Officer.
He's letting Gillie the Giraffe go first.

"Thank you, PC Barry."

Horace the Horse helps
Lino the Lion wash the
windows of the library.

"Stop!" calls Barry.
"That's not safe."

Eric the Elephant is a
firefighter. He lends his
ladder to Lino.

Yes, everyone stops to help
in Opposite Town.

Well, everyone except
Harry the Hare.

Harry never stops.

He runs everywhere.
He runs into Barry.
He runs into Eric.
He runs into the ladder.

Lino loses his balance and drops the bucket on PC Barry's head.

"Why are you always in a rush?" sighs Barry the Bear.

Harry is rushing home to watch the motor racing on television. It's his favourite sport.

"On no," says Harry. "The TV's broken."

Harry has an idea. He can watch the race with his best friend, Toto the Tortoise, who lives at the opposite end of Opposite Town.

Whoooooosh!

Harry runs all the way.

Toto is watching something different on the TV.
He prefers golf.

Harry thinks golf is too slow, so he starts looking for the remote control.

Can you see where it is?

It’s a very exciting moment for fans of golf, but all Harry can think of is the motor racing, so he changes the channel.

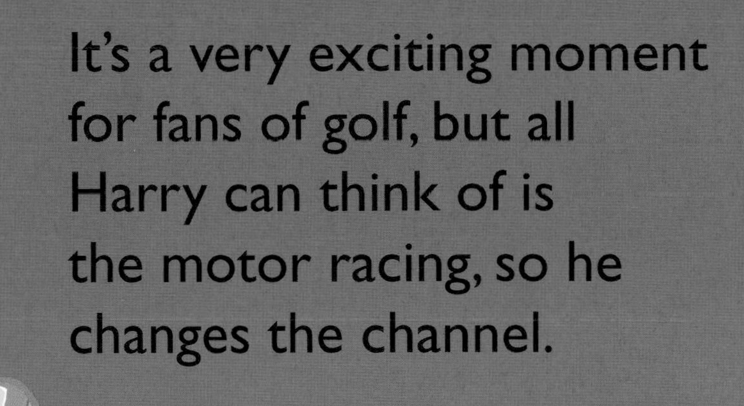

How do you think that makes Toto feel?

As the race gets underway, Harry becomes very excited and starts to jump

up

and

down.

Harry decides he wants to be a racing driver too and heads for his shed...

Hares really like inventing things.
What do you think Harry is making?

It’s a go-kart. Harry wants to be the fastest hare on four wheels.

Toto wants to tell his friend about road safety, but Harry doesn’t listen and rushes off to Opposite Mountain.

Harry climbs up to the top so he can race down to the bottom and speed into town.

Count down with Harry **3,2,1**

Go-go-go-go-go-go!

Harry speeds **up** Short Street

and **down** Long Street,

right into the middle
of Opposite Town.

When he gets to the traffic lights, Harry doesn't know what to do.

Everyone shouts, **"Stop!"**

Harry is very naughty and doesn't listen. He decides to **go!**

A big lorry is coming the opposite way.
The driver honks the horn to warn Harry.

Beep!

Harry brakes as quickly as he can. The go-kart stops just in time but Harry keeps on going.

Everyone runs to see how Harry is.
But he isn't on the ground.

Can you see Harry?

"I'm up here!" shouts Harry.
Harry is stuck in a tree.

"Don't worry," calls PC Barry.
"We'll get you down from there."

"But how?" wonders Gillie the Giraffe. "Even I'm not tall enough."

Now it's your turn to help.

Harry is stuck up a tree. Who do you think can help?

Is it Horace the Horse,
Eric the Elephant
or Gillie the Giraffe?

Who is the firefighter in Opposite Town?

It's Eric the Elephant.

"I'm on my way!" he calls.

Nee-nar, nee-nar goes his fire engine as he races to rescue Harry.

Eric goes **up** in his lift

so that Harry
can come

down.

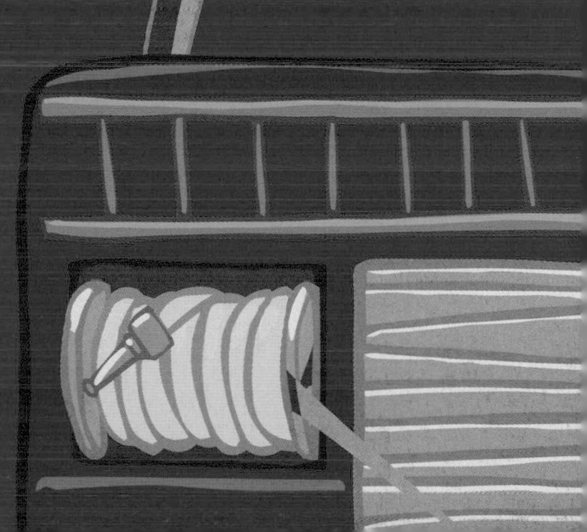

Now Harry wants to find his go-kart and race back home.

"Stop!" shouts PC Barry the Bear.

PC Barry thinks Harry needs a driving lesson first.

At the driving school, PC Barry explains that there are lots of signs on the road to help keep us safe. He shows Harry and Toto a game they can play.

Red for stop

Green for go

First PC Barry tells them to run around. When he holds up a red card they have to stop. Then, when he holds up a green card, they can go again.

Why don't you try?

Harry and Toto keep playing the game until they remember the rules.

"Well done," says PC Barry, "you can go home now."

Back at Toto's house, Toto is enjoying the golf until Harry tries to change the channel again.

"Stop," says Toto. "I don't like motor racing. If you want to watch it, go back to your house."

"Well, I don't like golf. I will go," announces Harry. So that's what Harry does.

On the way home, Harry stops and thinks. Being with his best friend is just as much fun as motor racing.

So he goes back to Toto's house and they have a milkshake. That's something they both like to do.

Harry and Toto are always finding opposites. If you enjoyed reading Stop and Go then look out for the other Opposite Stories.

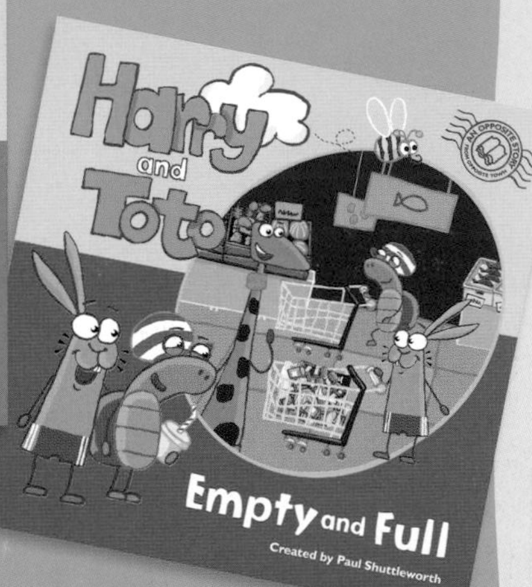